PRETEND YOU'RE A CAT

By JEAN MARZOLLO

Pictures by JERRY PINKNEY

A Puffin Pied Piper

PUFFIN PIED PIPER BOOKS
Published by the Penguin Group
Penguin Books USA Inc., 375 Hudson Street, New York, New York, 10014, U.S.A.
Penguin Books Ltd, 27 Wrights Lane, London W8 5TZ, England
Penguin Books Australia Ltd, Ringwood, Victoria, Australia
Penguin Books Canada Ltd, 10 Alcorn Avenue, Toronto, Ontario, Canada M4V 3B2
Penguin Books (N.Z.) Ltd, 182–190 Wairau Road, Auckland 10, New Zealand
Penguin Books Ltd, Registered Offices: Harmondsworth, Middlesex, England

Originally published in hardcover by
Dial Books for Young Readers
A Division of Penguin Books USA Inc.

Library of Congress Catalog Card Number: 89-34546
Printed in Hong Kong
First Puffin Pied Piper Printing 1997
ISBN 0-14-055993-0
1 3 5 7 9 10 8 6 4 2

A Pied Piper Book is a registered trademark of
Dial Books for Young Readers,
a division of Penguin Books USA Inc.,
® TM 1,163,686 and ® TM 1,054,312.

The full-color artwork was prepared using pencil, colored pencils,
and watercolor. It was then color-separated and reproduced as red,
blue, yellow, and black halftones.

PRETEND YOU'RE A CAT
is also available in hardcover from
Dial Books for Young Readers.

Can you climb?
Can you leap?
Can you stretch?
Can you sleep?

Can you hiss?
Can you scat?
Can you purr
Like a cat?

What else can you do like a cat?

Can you bark?
Can you beg?
Can you scratch
With your leg?

Can you fetch?
Can you roll?
Can you dig
In a hole?

What else can you do like a dog?

Can you jump?
Can you leap?
Can you swim
As you sleep?

Can you nibble
And look
At a worm
On a hook?

What else can you do like a fish?

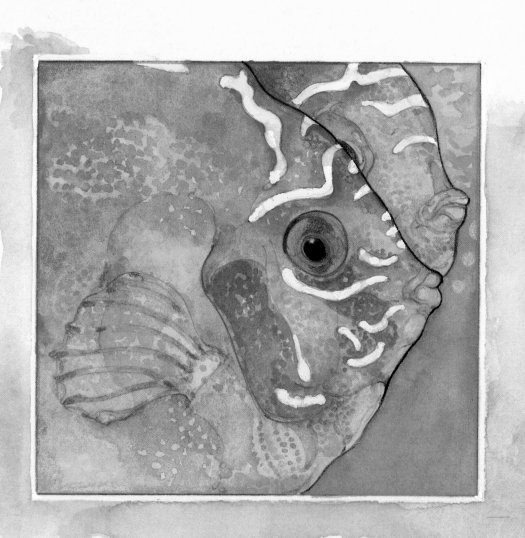

Can you fly?
Can you buzz?
Are you covered
With fuzz?

Can you land
On my knee?
Can you sting
Like a bee?

What else can you do like a bee?

Can you peck?
Can you pick
At a shell
Like a chick?

Can you scratch?
Can you cheep?
Can you hop?
Can you peep?

What else can you do like a chick?

Can you perch?
Can you fly?
Can you soar
In the sky?

Can you chirp?
Can you tweet?
Can you sing
With a beat?

What else can you do like a bird?

Can you chatter
And flee?
Disappear
In a tree?

Can you run?
Can you twirl?
Can you leap
Like a squirrel?

What else can you do like a squirrel?

Are you pink
As a bud?
Can you lie
In the mud?

Can you root?
Can you dig?
Can you snort
Like a pig?

What else can you do like a pig?

Can you chew?
Can you munch?
Can you moo
During lunch?

Can you drink
from a pail?
Touch your ear
With your tail?

What else can you do like a cow?

Can you snort?
Can you neigh?
Can you eat
Grain and hay?

Can you open
The gate?
Can you run
With your mate?

What else can you do like a horse?

Can you balance
A ball
On your nose
And not fall?

Can you dive
For your meal?
Can you bark
Like a seal?

What else can you do like a seal?

Can you wiggle
And glide?
Can you slither
And slide?

Can you head
For the lake?
Can you swim
Like a snake?

What else can you do like a snake?

Are you big?
Are you brave?
Can you sleep
In a cave?

Can you sniff
At the air?
Can you roar
Like a bear?

What else can you do like a bear?